A
PUSSYCAT'S
CHRISTMAS

For Tyler - *A.M.*

A Pussycat's Christmas
Text copyright 1949 Margaret Wise Brown
Text copyright renewed 1977 by Roberta Brown Rauch
Illustrations copyright © 1994 Anne Mortimer

First published in Great Britain in 1994 by
Frances Lincoln Limited, 4 Torriano Mews
Torriano Avenue, London NW5 2RZ

This edition first published in the United States in 1994 by
HarperCollins Publishers, Inc.

Published by arrangement with HarperCollins Publishers, Inc.,
New York, New York, U.S.A.

British Library Cataloguing in Publication Data
available on request

ISBN 0-7112-0872-7

Set in Garamond Book

Printed and bound in Italy

1 3 5 7 9 8 6 4 2

A PUSSYCAT'S CHRISTMAS

Margaret Wise Brown
Illustrated by Anne Mortimer

FRANCES LINCOLN

It was Christmas. How could you tell?
Was the snow falling?
No.
The little cat Pussycat knew that
Christmas was coming.
The ice tinkled when it broke on the
frozen mud puddles.
The cold air made her hair
stand straight up in the air.
And the air smelled just as it did last year.

What did it smell like?
Could she smell Christmas trees?

Of course she could.

And tangerines?

And Christmas greens?

And holly?

And could she hear the crackle and slip
of white tissue paper?

And red tissue paper?

She certainly could.

Tissue paper rustled.

Nuts cracked.

Scissors cut.

Brrrrr.

There wasn't a flake of snow in the sky.

But the sky was dark and low,

and there was the dark smell of winter air
    before snow.

And then,
    click,
the street lights clicked on all over the town.

And as the heavens turned dark
beyond the window,
    one
        by
            one
the snowflakes began to fall out of the sky.

How did little Pussycat know?
Could she hear the snow?

Sshshhhhhhhhssss.

She certainly could.

And she ran right out into the snow storm.

For if there was anything

that this little cat loved,

it was the cold, dry, fresh, white,

wild, and feathery, powdery snow.

She went pouncing around in it,

bouncing around in joy.

And she ate some of it.

And she rolled in it and dug in it

and played with it.

And then she stood up all white

with snow —

very still.

For it was very quiet,

very quiet.

First there was no sound.
And then there was some.
For when everything is quiet,
 you can hear things far away.
 From the sky with a sound
 like steady whispering
came the snow — that sound of snow.

Then the wind rattled the black branches.
 It was time for Pussycat
 to go into the house.

 For little cats do not like the wind.
 They usually don't like snow,
 but this little cat did.

All the smells of the earth that she knew
    were frozen and buried in the white snow.
The world was very quiet and very mysterious.
Even footsteps were quiet.
Pussycat didn't go in right away
because through the wind and the falling snow
    she heard something.

She stood very still and stretched her ears
    there in the whitened darkness.
        And soon she heard it
        coming from far away,
            away up the snowy road.

        Ding, ding, ding, ding,
        Jingle, jingle, jingle, ding.

    What was it?
    She heard it going by
        in the white falling snow.

She saw it!
She saw the sleigh go jingling by.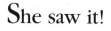

Then Pussycat miaowed at her window-pane.
And she heard footsteps coming to let her in.
They always let her in right away
because they didn't want her to get cold
   and they liked to have her in the house.

She walked right into the living-room
      where she could smell the sharp tangy smell
         of the Christmas tree and candles
   and nuts and raisins
and apples and tangerines.

But they shouldn't have let her stay
in the living-room
where they were wrapping up packages
   and hanging things on the tree.

And this is why.

Pussycat pounced.

She pounced on everything.

And she waited to pounce with shining eyes
and switching tail.

She waited with shining eyes
for something to fall,
to tinkle, to crash, and to break.

She batted the Christmas tree balls
with her paw.
Tore at the tissue paper
and pulled the bows off
the packages.

So they put her out
in the hall
and closed
the glass doors.

Pussycat lay down and purred by the fire.
She lifted her ears and she listened.
There was a sound of crackling.
  Shhhhh, shhhhh, crackle.
      What was that? Was it the fire?

      Always there was the sound of snow
        hissing against the window-pane.

There was a tiny tinkle little *pop*,
as something fell from the Christmas tree
    and shivered into a million splinters of light.
That was wonderful.

The lights gleamed in Pussycat's eyes.
Then
      bang bang bang.
What was that?
Someone was hanging up
    the Christmas stockings.

Everyone came out and stepped over
and around the little cat
and put on coats and boots
and mufflers and hats
    and laughed and shuffled about.

They kissed each other under the mistletoe.
Then off they went to church.

Suddenly and quietly far off in the night
    Pussycat could hear

Ding dong, ding dong,
    ding dong, ding dong.

    The snow had stopped.
And there was only the smell
of the Christmas tree
    filling the house.

And silence.

Then softly at first but distinct in the night
she heard people walking
from window to window —
    the dark carol-singers on the white snow.

Through the still air their voices
came to her listening ears —
over the silence of the frozen snow
in the silence of the moonlight
in the silence of the night
in the silence of the bright stars
    high in the sky

Silent night, holy night,
    All is calm, all is bright...

And as the little Pussycat
purred and purred by the fire,
she heard in the distance the music
    fading far down the road.

Then she pushed open
the living-room door with her paw
and there in the silent house
   was the Christmas tree.
It sparkled and glistened with lights,
   gold and silver and blue,
      the light of rubies and emeralds,
         shining like no tree that any cat
            had ever seen in the woods.

This to Pussycat was Christmas Eve.